The Adventures of Ears O'Fluffin, Pet PI

Volume 1

Monica Yoknis

This is a work of fiction, any resemblance to anyone, living or dead, is purely coincidental...and highly unlikely...these are animals, after all. While I did draw inspiration from experiences others have had with their house rabbits, any resemblance to actual events is unintentional.

ISBN: 978-0-692-92964-3

This book is dedicated to my bunny, Peaches, for introducing me to the wonderful world of House Rabbits. And to Dustin Campbell, creator of Bunnyzine, for giving me a publishing platform and encouraging me to keep writing the stories.

The Case of the Disappearing Willow Ball

I plopped into my chair with a sigh and pulled open my desk drawer. Inside were my two best friends, a pop gun that I keep loaded, and a bottle of carrot juice that keeps me loaded. I set the bottle on the desk and pulled out a shot glass. The detecting business has been slow, of late, but I keep hoping for a case. I have some hope that the new upgrade to my office will help bring in the clients. The hoomin gave me a nice remodel. The back door will come in handy, and the window in front adds a nice touch. I hung my shingle out right after I finished inspecting the new place. Yes, that's me, Ears O'Fluffin, Pet PI. Now all I needed was a case to investigate, and here I am pouring myself a shot of carrot and it's not even 10:30 in the morning.

Holy hares, was that a knock at the door? Yes, it was! I quickly stowed the bottle and glass as I beckoned, "Come in!" In walked a very prim blue Dutch lady. She'd be beautiful if she didn't look so drawn and wary. Behind her was a handsome white lionhead, apparently her husbun. "Have a seat, folks, what can I do for you?"

"My name is Tuffy," the lionhead offered. "And this is my wife, Muffy."

"Pleased to meet you sir, ma'am."

"We need your help." Tuffy paused to put a paw on his wife's shoulder. "It's our willow ball, you see, it's been stolen."

"It was there last night, Mr O'Fluffin, I'm sure of it," Muffy squeaked. "Then this morning, gone!" She buried her face in her paws.

"I looked everywhere in our room, and there was no sign of it. I even slipped out when the hoomin brought our breakfast. I made it all the way into the kitchen before she scooped me up, but I didn't see it anywhere," Tuffy closed his eyes for a moment. "It's such a nice willow ball, you see. Big and crunchy, and it rolls so well."

"I understand," I assured them, thinking of my own favorite toy. "I'd be happy to help you folks. Now, I do want to let you know that my standard fee for missing items is one pineapple chunk per hour...."

"Of course, that seems reasonable," Tuffy nodded. "Do you prefer dried or fresh?"

"Whichever is easiest for you folks."

"Oh, thank you, Detective. Do you really think you can find it?" Muffy pleaded.

"Well, I can certainly find out what happened to it. If it is recoverable, be assured I will get it back to you," I smiled confidently. "First, I'd like to see the scene of the crime, if you don't mind."

I went with Muffy and Tuffy to their Bunroom. Wow, nice digs! They even had one of those fancy Ikea beds. Not that I mind my hammock, but dang that bed looked cozy. I asked them to show me where they had left the willow ball the night before.

"We always roll it into this corner after dinner," Muffy informed me. There were a few other toys in the same corner.

"Is anything else missing?" I asked, looking at Tuffy.

"Well, let me see," he examined each toy. "No, sir, they are all here. Only the willow ball is gone."

"Oh dear," Muffy stifled a sob.

"Alright, Tuffy, take your wife over for some hay. I'll start my search in this room," I took off my hat and coat. "I will be looking for the tiniest clues, so it would be best if you both stayed in your hay corner."

"Certainly, we will do our best to stay out of the way," Tuffy gently steered his wife into the far corner of the room.

I spent a good long time searching the Bunroom. What was most interesting was what I didn't find.

The place was spotless. No hay on the floor, and no stray pooties anywhere. It looked like a hoomin had just been through with a hoover monster. Scary as those things may be, I've yet to see one that could suck up a willow ball. Of course, that didn't mean the the hoomin didn't abscond with the beloved ball. My own hoomin has a strange tendency to take away toys before I'm done bunstructing them. I needed to search the rest of the house. A quick periscope told me my clients were cuddled together in their litter box. Not wanting to intrude on their private moments, I let myself out of the room. The rest of the ground floor was just as disturbingly clean as the Bunroom. Even the trash cans were empty. I tried to get into the kitchen trash, but my two pounds couldn't budge the foot pedal. I'll blame the vet for that. Humph, diet my fluffy butt! A knock on the side of the can sounded too hollow to make much more effort worth while, so I headed up the stairs.

The first room I ventured into was neat, tidy, and elegantly appointed. Must be an adult's room. I caught the slight sweet scent of dried willow and followed it to the bedside table. There, partly hidden under the table was a bent twig of willow. Definitely part of the missing ball. I examined it closely, and decided that this had been crushed, not chewed. All bunnies know that sickening crunch of a

hoomin stepping on a willow ball. Almost always
followed by a few colorful epithets, an apology, and
"If you'd put your toys away...."

"Now, how did you get up here?" I asked the twig.

"I stole it," a smooth baritone answered as a
shadow fell over me. I looked up to see an
excessively floofy white cat peering over the edge of
the bed.

"Huh," I replied trying to hide my surprise. "I
didn't know they made angora cats."

"You," he growled, "do not belong here."

"I've been..."

"Rabbits are not allowed upstairs." He pulled
himself into a crouch, and stared intently into my
eyes. "And you are a stranger here."

I dropped the twig and bolted a split second before
he pounced. I didn't really pay as much attention to
where I was going as I should have, and ended up in
a bathroom. The feline fluff ball stayed right on my
pouf, so I scooted behind the toilet, then ran into the
trashcan hoping to push it in his way. The two
second delay gave me a chance to find my way back
to the hallway. I flew down the stairs and turned
towards the safety of the bunroom, only to find the
way blocked by another cat. A skinny red thing, of a
breed I've never seen before. My many hours of
binky practice served me well as I hopped straight
up and turned mid-air. I hit the ground running and

sprinted for the nearest open door. I skidded into
the room and slammed the door closed behind me.
A heavy thud from the other side knocked me back.
Ha! Cat ran into the door.

I didn't take the time to gloat, but pushed a rolling
office chair against the door. It wasn't a perfect
solution, but it would have to do. Looking around, I
saw a nice tight spot under a printer cart and dove
in to catch my breath. I made myself as small as I
could, closed my eyes, and willed my heart to stay in
my chest. I could hear the cats on the other side of
the door meowing, taunting me. I chose to ignore
them and rest.

As soon as I was sure my heart and lungs were
keeping their places, I stretched and started looking
around. Tucked away in a corner was a cardboard
box, its top was cross folded to keep it closed. This
left enough of an opening for the sweet smell of
dried willow, among other delights, to waft out and
reach my twitchy booplesnoot. I tested the top to
see if it would hold me. It seemed firm enough, so I
hopped up for a closer look. The return address
label was from a well known bunny toy store. A
whisker test suggested I could squeeze into the box,
and it looked shallow enough for me to be able to get
back out, so I dove into the box. The first half went
in well enough, but the rear end.... Let's just say I
was very glad no one was around to see my fluffy

white butt sticking straight up in the air. My hoomin's words replayed themselves in my head, "O'Fluffin, buddy, you really need to ease up on the cookies and carrot juice!" I hated to admit he might have been right, so I didn't. After a few wiggles, gravity won over friction and I was in the box. It was too dark in the box to see anything, but my sniffer lead me to a giant willow ball. As I traced the dimensions of the ball with my paws, I realized it was roughly as big as I was.

"Hoo boy!" I looked up at the opening, trying to gauge the likelihood of getting the ball out without opening the box. "Um, yeah, I'm gonna go with no." Periscoping up, I pushed on the cardboard flaps. They were too stiff, and too high up to push open from inside. I moved a treat box under the hole and used it to get my front half out of the box. Working against gravity, it took considerably more wiggling to get my booty out. Once out, I set my back toes on the edge of the box, and gripped the edge of the flap with my front paws. Then I pulled as hard as I could. Just when I thought the flap was going to pop out, it snapped back down so fast I didn't have a chance to let go. I found myself flying forward toward the wall, so I started to roll myself into a ball. I hit the wall with my back, and slid down to the floor, wedged between the side of the box and the wall. I was stuck. On my head. The situation called for profanity, and I used some. I will not apologize.

I flailed my thumpers around until my butt slid down to the floor. I shimmied my way backwards to get out of the crevice, then looked around to make sure I was still alone. Thankful that no one had witnessed any of that, I kicked the offending box. The noise drew more derisive meows from the cats on the other side of the door. Well, at least I still knew where they were.

I plopped onto my pouf, stretched my thumpers out in front of me, rested my elbows on my knees, and my chin on my paws. This is my best thinking pose, and it did me well this time. Given the size of the willow ball, even if I could get it out of the box, there was no way I could heft it up to the window. I could probably roll it around to the pet flap in the back door, but I can't be sure I could get it up and into the hole, if it would even fit through. Then there was the question of how Muffy and Tuffy's hoomins would react to finding the new ball magically in the bunroom. I didn't want to get my clients in trouble. Given all that, I decided to leave the ball where it was and let my clients know what happened to the old ball, and assure them that a new ball was forthcoming. They would just have to accept that.

I stood up and stretched as far as I could, then looked around to make sure nothing was terribly out of place. The only thing I had really moved was

12

the chair. I considered moving it back, but the cats started pounding and scratching on the door again. Best to leave the chair in place. A hoomin would be able to move it as he opened the door. Let them puzzle about how it had gotten there.

I hopped from one piece of furniture to another, working my way up to the window. I was delighted to realize that it was one of those garden-level rooms, so I didn't have far to fall. The window opened easily enough, and I slipped out onto the exterior ledge. My hoomin would freak if he saw me doing this, he always does when I practice on the entertainment cabinet. I pushed the window closed, and just left it unlocked. Most hoomins would assume they had forgotten to lock it, so I wasn't worried about the buns getting in trouble for that.

I dropped down to the ground and ran around the house to the pet door. I waited for a while to make sure the cats hadn't had enough genius to figure I'd slipped out. With no sign of them, I quietly snuck in through the flap and tiptoed across the kitchen floor. From the door to the dining room, I could see the door to the bunroom. It was about 10 yards. Not a long way, but I was already tired. The question then was, do I sprint and risk the cats hearing me? Or do I tiptoe and risk the time it would take to get there? I could hear them still shouting insults through the door, so I chose to go for the sprint and get to a safer place.

I set myself into a squat, took a few deep breaths, and launched myself across the dining and living rooms. My paws barely touched the floor as I flew through the house. My hoomin loves it when I do that at home, so I get a lot of practice in...yet somehow have an enlarged posterior. Ahh, it must be muscle, not fat. The vet can gnaw on that idea for a while!

The cats may not have heard me running, but Tuffy sure did. He was there waiting with the door open for me, and closed it tight behind me. Muffy was waiting in the middle of the room, wringing her paws.

"Oh my goodness! Mr O'Fluffin, are you alright?" she squeaked.

"Yes, ma'am," I assured her. "I'm a bit winded, but fine otherwise."

"We heard the cats chasing you through the house. I'm so sorry, I should have told you about them!" Tuffy apologized.

"No, no, don't worry about it," I shook my head. "I should have asked about other residents. That is completely my fault. Now let me tell you what I learned...." I explained the whole thing, about finding the crushed twig, the cat admitting he stole the ball, and about finding a new ball in the office. "I'm certain they will be giving you the new ball as soon as they can." They both agreed that made sense, given their hoomin's recent behavior.

I looked at my watch. Then I looked again, 3:30 pm?! No wonder I was tired and hungry! "Let's see, that's five hours of investigation, so that's five pineapple chunks." Muffy hopped off to a corner to count out my payment, and I slipped back into my hat and coat. She came back with a pouch, really just a scrap of fabric tied with a piece of sisal string. She opened it on the floor to let me see the five pieces of dried pineapple. "These are freeze dried, so they travel very well," she explained as she retied the bundle.

I thanked her for the pineapple, and tucked the pouch into a pocket. Tuffy offered to walk me to the back door, assuring me that the cats would not bother me with him there. I thanked him, shook Muffy's paw, and went with her husbun through the house into the kitchen. There was no sign of the cats anywhere, a fact for which I was quite grateful.

"Thank you again, Mr O'Fluffin, and be sure we will recommend you to all our friends," Tuffy held out his paw.

"Thank you, I always welcome referrals," I shook his paw, and hopped out the pet door.

Halfway home, I pulled out a pineapple piece. Wow, how do I convince my hoomin to get those?!

Back in my office, I hung up my coat and hat. I closed up the office, visited my litter box, water dish, and pellet bowl. In that order. I dragged myself to my bed, flopped onto my side, and fell fast asleep.

The Mystery of the Empty Treat Jar

I was sitting at my desk, staring at the last page I'd written from the willow ball adventure. I turned to a blank page, and wondered if this gig with Bunnyzine would pay out. Last night, my hoomin laughed and showed me the latest article from Mrs Obi. Why anyone would open a store just for perfume is beyond me, but that's the female mind for ya.

Contemplating the bizarre nature of dames, I absently reached into my desk drawer. My paw had just touched the bottle of carrot juice when there was a knock at the door. Before I could say anything, the door swung open, and the biggest rabbit I've ever seen poked his head in.

"Mr O'Fluffin?" the giant asked.

"Yes, I..." before I could suggest that I join him outside, the world's biggest rabbit pushed into my office. He fit ok, until his hips got stuck. He sighed, wiggled his massive cotton bottom, and popped through the door. My office, which had always felt spacious, was now very crowded. I sat in my chair, marveling that this bun's head was as big as my whole body. I decided that I definitely did not want to be thumped by this guy. He seemed tired and worried. "How can I help you, sir?"

"I hope you can help me," he sighed. "My name is Peanut. I'm an only bun, but my hoomin takes very good care of me." He stopped, apparently reflecting on his hoomin.

"I'm glad you have a good hoomin," I prodded.

"Me too." He took a deep breath and continued. "Last night, I asked my hoomin for a treat, and she said they were all gone. That has never happened before, and I remember that morning the jar was almost full. I know I didn't eat them. I didn't believe her, so I insisted. She showed me the jar. It was empty, Mr O'Fluffin, completely empty!"

"I'm sure I can help you, Peanut. Let's head to the scene and I'll start investigating right away," I reached behind me for my hat and coat while my new client wiggled himself out the door.

Peanut had full run of a spacious two-story house. His primary area was a living room with plush tan carpet. I could feel my paws sinking into the lush pile. Sure it looks nice, but I prefer my hoomin's

choice of a tight low-pile rug. Much easier to run on.
The enormous kitchen had enough cabinets to store
a lifetime worth of treats, but of course hoomins
aren't bright enough to use them for that. The floor
here was a dark slate tile, nice and cool, felt
wonderful on the thumpers.

My client was able to use his claws (talons!) to pry
open the pantry door. The bottom cupboard opened
easliy, revealing a translucent plastic bin, and a lot of
empty space.

"That's where my treats are kept," he gestured to
the bin.

"I understand, thank you. You head off to rest or
play, and I'll look around," I put a reassuring paw on
his shoulder. He nodded and plodded off into the
living room. I took off my hat and coat, and laid
them neatly on the edge of the cupboard floor. My
first thought was that an intruder of the small and
naked-tailed variety might have absconded with the
precious treats, so I hopped up into the cabinet to
look for evidence. This was easliy the cleanest
cabinet I'd ever been in, not a crumb, and hardly a
speck of dust. Oddly enough, this is not evidence
against my mouse idea. The hoomin, having found
the treats missing, would likely have cleaned up
after the thief. Even my hoomin, who is not the
tidiest in the world, cleans up mouse leavings. What
did argue against mice was the complete lack of an

access hole. Nor was there evidence of a recent
repair or filling of a hole.

I tried to examine the treat bin, but it fit so closely
in the cabinet, that I couldn't get a good look. Given
how large it was (giant rabbits must eat giant
treats), I opted to push it out, rather than pull it and
have it fall on me. I hopped back to the pantry floor
to study the bin. It was a typical Bunnerware treat
container, except for the atypical size. The lid,
however, was far more interesting. It was obvious
that something had pried the lid off. Something that
had large teeth. Huge teeth. I could fit my entire
toe...not claw, TOE...in one of the tooth marks. And
have room to wiggle said toe. I could feel the hairs
along my spine start to stand up as my brain, against
my will, started concocting an image of the creature
that possessed such teeth. I really did not like where
my brain, despite my arguments, was going with
those images. I failed to suppress a shudder.

I spent a few moments collecting myself, sniffing
and listening intently. When I was sure there was
no giant monster about to spring on me, I took a
deep breath and started investigating the rest of the
pantry. I was able to get the other lower cabinets
open, but found nothing of interest.

I wanted to put the treat bin back into the cabinet,
but decided to wait and have Peanut help me. It's
not often I come across a disadvantage to being a

dwarf bun, but hefting giant jars into cabinets certainly counts. The jar could wait.

The image of those huge tooth marks flashed before me as I started to cross the threshold into the kitchen. I paused and scanned the room carefully. Once I was satisfied that there were no monsters, I scanned again for the most likely place to begin searching for clues. In the far corner, I saw a trio of plastic bins. The writing on them, "Paper", "Plastic", and "Mixed", was enough to tell me what the bins would hold. My hoomin has four recycle bins. I could see the top of the stack in the "Paper" bin, and it looked like something had been shredded. Possibly by the same ginormous teeth that had damaged Peanut's treat jar.

I hopped over to the bin and periscoped up to examine the mangled box. It was a dog treat box. There wasn't much left of it, but it still held the scent of dog breath. It wasn't hard to imagine what had happened: the hoomin likely kept the dog treat box in the same cabinet as Peanut's treat jar. Dog got into the cupboard, tore up the box, and feasted on his treats. Still hungry (or possibly on a treat high), he then worked the lid off the Bunnerware jar, and gobbled those up, too.

I didn't want to go to my client with only "the dog did it", so I looked around for any evidence that the hoomin planned to replace the stolen treats. My eyes finally rested on a magnetic notepad stuck to the door of the freezer. I hadn't seen one of these freezer-over-fridge types in a while, but these hoomins had one. That meant that I had a slightly better chance of getting to the notepad, as the top of the fridge door offered a ledge for me to stand on.

I could see that the notepad was currently blank, but if I moved just right, the light played across the indentations from the previous page. It looked like a list. I hopped back into the pantry for my hat and coat. The pencil stub I keep in my pocket would be perfect for rubbing over the indented paper. I suspected that there would be treats on the list, but I wanted to be sure. Peanut seemed nervous enough, I thought he could really use some certainty about this. Besides, nobun likes to be without treats for long.

Most hoomin kitchens have a stack of drawers on one side of the fridge, and this kitchen was no exception. I pulled out the bottom drawer as far as I could, hopped up, then pulled out the next drawer. I continued up, turning the drawers into a set of bunny stairs, until I reached the counter. Then I used the storage boxes and jars to work my way up to the level of the top of the fridge door. Gripping the rubber seal on the side of the freezer door, I flattened my fluffy tummy against the front of the door, and planted my toes on the top of the fridge door. Keeping my grip on the side, I shuffled and stretched across to the notepad. I tried to pull the pad off, but the magnet was surprisingly strong. It did slide, though, so I pulled it closer to the side so I could get better leverage. I tensed up and put all my muscles to work on pulling the notepad away from the door. Finally, it popped off, but it swung toward me and bonked me on the head before falling to the floor.

The knock on my head pushed me away from the surface of the door, and I felt my claws lose grip of the rubber seal. I scrambled to regain my balance and my hold on the door, but gravity won and I felt my thumpers skid on the slick surface as I started to fall.

There was a brief moment of feeling weightless, suspended in the air above the kitchen floor. Then I felt gravity's tug, and I twisted myself to land on my feet. I did okay, for the most part. I did land a little hard on my left thumper, and could feel the tendon pop as it sprained. I rolled onto my right side to get pressure off the injury, and laid there for a couple minutes gently working out the angry tissue. Then I tried to stand. Three feet were alright, but that one did not like having weight on it.

I hopped carefully over to my coat and put the pencil stub in my mouth, then slowly made my way to the fallen note pad. I rubbed the side of the pencil lead lightly across the indented paper, and smiled as a grocery list emerged. One of the items listed was "bunny treats". I smiled, pulled the sheet off the pad, and slid the pad to the base of the fridge. The hoomin would think it had just slid off the door onto the floor. Carrying pencil and paper back to my coat, I got dressed and started the journey into the living room to find my client. I made a point to start putting more weight on the sore foot, and by the time I reached Peanut, I was walking close to normal.

Peanut was relieved to see me. He'd heard me hit the floor, but wasn't sure what he should do. I told him about my fall, and he apologized profusely. I reassured him that I was fine, and told him I needed help getting the jar back in the cabinet. He noticed the limp as we made our way back to the kitchen. I showed him the tooth marks on the jar lid, and told him about the dog treat box. I could almost see the light bulb turn on in his head, and he explained that his doggy brofur does have a very bad sweet tooth. We maneuvered the jar back into the cabinet and closed the door.

As we left the pantry, Peanut thanked me and asked what he owed me. I thought for a couple seconds, then told him half a carrot. He bounced over to the fridge, closed the drawers I'd forgotten were open, wedged himself against them, and

pushed on the edge of the fridge door. It swung
open, and Peanut stretched up to the bottom shelf
where a bag of carrots was conveniently placed. He
pulled out the biggest carrot I've ever seen. I guess
giant rabbits need giant carrots. He handed it to me
as the fridge door swung shut behind him. I took it
in both paws, but it was twice as long as I was even
when I stretched out as far as I could go.

"Um," I said, "I can accept a quarter of a carrot. I've
never seen one this big." Peanut giggled and insisted
I take the whole thing. When I protested, he insisted
because I'd gotten hurt. Then he offered to help me
get home. I tried to say I'd be okay, but he told me I
didn't have a choice, that he would help me get
home.

He helped me get the massive carrot into my office,
and made sure I was comfortable. I usually don't let
anybun fuss over me, but you don't argue with a
giant rabbit. He thanked me profusely again, then
binkied as he set off for home. I nibbled a bit of the
huge carrot, wiggled out of my hat and coat, then
made my way to my bed. I flopped on my right side,
adjusted my left thumper till it was comfortable,
then fell fast asleep.

The Adventure of the Missing Vet Records

The day after my adventures with Peanut the Giant and his hoomin's rock-hard kitchen floor, I found myself limping to breakfast. I tried to hide it, not wanting my hoomin to worry, but I was unsuccessful. He patted my head while I ate and asked if I was OK. I just kept eating, hoping he'd think I'd just slept funny. It seemed to work, since he went off to his office. Halfway from the breakfast dish to my office, I decided to spend the day closer to my bed and litter box.

My hoomin usually will peek into my office a few times a day to make sure all is well, and tell me not to worry, that a new client was sure to come by soon enough. He isn't used to seeing me in bed during the day, but I tried to stay as flopped as I could. I wanted him to think I just wanted a day off. I discovered that my attempts at nonchalance failed, however, when I heard my hoomin on the phone.

"Hello, I need to make an appointment for Ears." I knew what that meant, the hoomin was calling the vet. "Today would be best...he's just not himself...I think he hurt his back leg, he's holding it stiffly and seemed to be favoring it at breakfast...no, he ate like normal, and his poops seem normal." Hmph, how would they like it if we told their doctors about the quality of their poops! "Yes...eleven o'clock is perfect, we'll be there." I scrambled to my feet and backed into my protest corner.

My hoomin came into the room with the carrier and a towel. He set the carrier on the dining table and arranged the towel on the bottom, then approached me. "Ok, little man, time to go see the doc about that leg." I grunted and backed further into my protest corner. "Nope, sorry, time to go." He reached down for me. Honestly, I don't mind it when he picks me up and holds me. I glare at him when he describes me as a cuddle bun, but honestly I can't really deny it. I just really didn't want to go to the vet. Just before he got to me, I thumped. Well, I tried to thump. I admit, it was pretty pathetic. And to make it worse, I accidentally let out a slight squeak. That earned me a light scolding. "There, see," he gave me one of those told-you-so looks, "there's something wrong with your thumper. I don't know what kind of trouble you got into on that last case, but I'm betting you hurt yourself." Ha! If he knew the kinds of adventures I had on those cases, he'd make me close up shop for good.

I won't bore all you good people with the ride to the vet's office. Honestly, I fumed the whole way. I tried to thump a couple more times, but never did get my point across. We had to sit in the waiting room for an exam room to open up. My hoomin looked into my carrier a few times, and I made sure to glare at him. He, as usual, told me I was "adorable" when I was mad. Yeah, hoomin, that really helps the situation, doesn't it? Once in the exam room, he let me out of the carrier. I was about to hop (hobble) into a protest corner, but he scooped me up for a cuddle. I won't lie, it's difficult to stay mad at them when they snuggle like that. Besides, the floor was cold. Don't judge me, I'm still a tough guy. Really.

The vet came in, tech in tow. While the vet greeted my hoomin and rubbed my nose, the tech set a scale on the counter, a nice plush towel on the scale, and zeroed the scale. My hoomin set me on the scale and the vet recorded the number. No, I will not tell you what it said, so don't ask! The vet took the rest of my vitals, then set about checking my feet. I don't like having my feet messed with. Not that I'm ticklish, or anything (I am not), I just prefer they be left alone. I will concede that I jumped when she got to the sore foot. I had been determined not to, but it just happened. The conclusion was that I needed an x-ray. I tried to argue, but my hoomin, being a bit of a worrier, agreed and arrangements were made for me to stay overnight for x-rays and observation. I got a nice parting cuddle, and a firm admonition to behave myself, before my hoomin put me back in the carrier. I thumped (tried to) as the tech carried me back to the hospital rooms.

I was snoozing warily in the metal enclosure, when a soft step caught my ear. I stayed motionless and listened. The nearly silent steps crossed the room and approached the wall of cages. There was a narrow ledge of cage floor that extended out beyond the wire doors. The hoomins used the ledge as an assist for getting critters in and out of the cages. now it was used for a different purpose. I felt the weight of the animal as it jumped from the floor and landed on the ledge. Aside from the vibration of the landing, there was only the soft hissing sound of furred paws on the smooth metal. It was my nose that told me the nature of this night time prowler. I'd seen the resident office cat before, but never actually met him.

I stayed still as the cat settled on the narrow ledge just outside my door. He waited in silence, listening, before whispering at me. "Detective O'Fluffin, are you awake?"

"Yes," I whispered back.

"If you're up to it, I could use your assistance with a problem."

I stood carefully, and hopped, three-legged, over to the cage door. "I'd be glad to help, if I can. What's the problem?" I don't generally work pro bono, but I was bored, and couldn't sleep anyway.

"Dr White is becoming frustrated, papers and supplies keep disappearing."

"A pack rat, maybe?"

"That was my original thought, and we do get wild rodents coming in, despite my best efforts, but there's no evidence that I can find of them getting into the office."

"Interesting." This did, indeed seem like a real puzzle, and I found that I was intrigued. "I'd like to see this office, if you'd be willing to help me get there."

"Certainly. I heard the doc saying that you needed to stay off that foot, and I don't want to be the reason you get into trouble with him. If you're not too proud to accept a lift, and can hang onto my back, I'll be happy to carry you around as needed."

I thought for a few seconds. I wasn't too keen on the idea of riding on a cat's back, but the mystery was too much to pass up over a bit of stung self esteem. I agreed to the cat's offer, and watched as he reached up and unclipped the cage door. He introduced himself as Baxter, and apologized that he had not properly introduced himself in the lobby.

He settled low on his belly so that I could carefully

climb onto his back. I got a firm grip around his neck, and was able to squeeze my knees into his side for stability. He moved smoothly along the ledge to a counter in the corner. A few short leaps from counter to chair, to floor, and we were gliding along to the doctor's private office.

The office was small and windowless. There was only an old metal desk and a rolling office chair to suggest that this was any kind of work space. Otherwise the room was crowded with filing cabinets. Three cabinets were the most prominent, bearing labels of "Dogs", "Cats", and "Exotics". Each drawer was then labeled with letters of the alphabet.

Baxter warned me to hold on, so I tightened my grip. He jumped onto the office chair, then onto the desk. I slid off his back when he lowered himself to his belly.

"This is where the papers are disappearing from."

"Right here, from the desktop?" No wonder the doc was getting frustrated.

"Right here. He would leave a file out to work on in the morning, and come back to find the folder empty. Sometimes the contents would be scattered around the desk, sometimes they would be gone completely."

"How long has this been happening?"

"About three months, now."

I hopped around the top of the desk, closely

examining everything. Had I known, I would have grabbed my magnifying glass as my hoomin picked me up. I didn't see any traces left by anyone other than some loose hairs Baxter had dropped. There was a hint of a scent I'd never encountered before, but it was too faint to get a good read. I stopped at the spot where the mystery smell was strongest, and asked Baxter to have a sniff. He admitted that he'd noticed it before, but gave up and came to me when he couldn't find an actual trail. After thinking a minute, his eyes lit up.

"It almost smells like something I've come across outside. There's a burrow out behind the building that has a similar smell, but it seems pretty empty. Kinda like whatever was in there hasn't been there in a long time."

I nodded, trying to imagine a scenario where a scent from an outside burrow made its way inside onto the top of a desk, and only the top of the desk. I'd settled myself into a nearly comfortable thinking loaf, twitching my nose rhythmically, when the slightest of drafts tickled an ear. I listened a moment and concluded that the ventilation system had turned itself on. I took a deep breath to settle back into my contemplations when that same mysterious scent triggered an alarm in my head. At first I thought it was from the surface of the desk, but this was different somehow. Fresher. I looked at Baxter to see if he'd caught it, too. He was looking at me with wide eyes. We both turned our gaze slowly up to the ceiling and sniffed. No doubt about it, the mystery smell was coming down from the air vent.

I closed my eyes and thought for a minute. There was no way we were getting into the vent system from the top of the doctor's desk, not without a rope, anyway. I asked Baxter if he knew where the heater was kept.

"There's a utility room in the back, but the door is locked."

I looked around the desk, and found a container of paper clips. I hopped over and fished through for the biggest clip. "Let me worry about the lock," I assured him as I tested the bend strength of the paper clip. "Yup, this one is perfect." I bent the clip into the most common shape for picking locks, and smiled at Baxter. He was grinning, and settled down so I could climb back on his back. I put the clip in my mouf, held carefully by my top and bottom incisors, and resumed my seat on Baxter's back.

We glided through the building, the only sound our passing made was the barely audible pat pat of kitty feet on the tile. After passing through the door at the far end of the hallway, we passed through a heavy steel fire door, and into some sort of loading bay. This room, with a bare concrete floor, was apparently used for storage. Baxter trotted past several banks of locked metal cabinets, then stopped at another heavy steel door. He had demonstrated a proficiency with opening the lever type knobs, so far, but I could see that the knob on this door included a lock.

I asked Baxter to put his front paws up on the door so I could get a look at the lock. I decided that I needed to adjust my lock pick, so I had him lower me to the floor. While I reconfigured my pick, Baxter considered how he was going to hold me up long enough to unlock the door. I already knew the best way, but he was able to figure it out, on his own.

"I guess you'll have to sit on my shoulders to reach that far?" he seemed doubtful that I'd agree to that.

"That'd be the most stable arrangement I can think of."

"Just be careful of that leg."

"Of course, no worries."

He crouched with his nose to the door right under the knob, and I wiggled myself into position on his shoulders. The ride up as he stood to his full height was more like I imagine a roller-coaster to be than I would have preferred, but it was necessary. Baxter set himself against the door, and assured me that he was stable, so I went to work on the lock. Those industrial locks fall into two categories, as far as I'm concerned. There are the really cheap easy ones,

and the really expensive hard ones. Thankfully, this
was a cheap lock, and I was able to get the door open
fairly quickly. The problem was that the door swung
out toward us, so Baxter had to back away to make
sure the Latch stayed open, but without dropping
me on the ground. Let's just say I was impressed
with his balance and reflexes.

I stayed on the floor while he pulled the door open,
then we slowly peered into the utility room. The
scent we caught in the office was stronger here, but
not strong enough to indicate the perp was present
at that moment. I hopped in on three legs, ears
cocked as far forward as they'd go, nose twitching to
catch even the faintest smell. We carefully eased
into the room towards the furnace. Just as we were
a hoomin foot away from the heater, there was a
knock on the side panel. We jumped back just in
time to avoid being smashed as the large metal
panel crashed to the floor in front of us.

We gazed intently into the dark cavity of the
furnace, listening as the sound of the crash
reverberated off the walls. Now the mystery scent
was almost overwhelming. The perp had to be
inside. Together, we stepped cautiously onto the
fallen panel, watching for any movement.

A pointy pink nose, sporting glorious silver
whiskers, poked out from the edge of the hole. Its
owner must have caught our scent, just as we had

its. Baxter glanced at me. I took that to mean he was deferring to me. Great, as if I knew what to do. I took a deep breath and mustered my most authoritative tone.

"Come out of there slowly, whoever you are."

The nose was followed by a long, tapering white snout. A black, nervous eye scanned the room, then fixed on us.

"I mean no harm, please don't tell the humans." The intruder sounded female, and was clearly frightened, but she also had long, needle like teeth. I glanced at Baxter. He nodded, so I continued.

"We won't tell them if we don't have to. Come on out, now."

She placed her hands on the bottom edge of the opening. It looked like she was wearing fingerless black opera gloves. As she crawled out of the opening, I could see that her body was covered by black and silver fur that shimmered in the dim light. Her ears were all black, and rounded like my Teddy bear's. Then came her tail. It was long, round, and naked, like a rat's. I searched my memory. I know I've seen pictures of such a creature, but it took me a while to recall the name.

"You're an opossum, aren't you?" I asked.

"Uh, yes, I am. My name is Violet"

Baxter finally spoke up, "You've been stealing the Doc's files?"

"Borrowing, really." She paused, "I just haven't figured out how to give them back, yet."

Baxter and I exchanged a glance. I shrugged, and turned back to the intruder. "But why? What could you possibly need them for?"

"I'm the local healer. I've been using the records as a treatment guide."

"And the supplies?" Baxter asked.

"I make sure to take only what I absolutely have to." She looked embarrassed by the supply thefts. "I know I don't have a way to return the supplies, but my patients bring in whatever lost coins they find, and I leave them around in the supply room."

Baxter chuckled, "Well, now that mystery has an explanation."

I smiled and shifted my weight in an effort to get comfortable. My sore leg was throbbing from all the activity. Baxter noticed and started to say something, but I cut him off to ask the opossum, "Do you have the papers with you, now?"

"I do. I had thought about dropping them from the vent onto the floor by the doctor's desk, but I heard you two in the office, so I decided to wait until later."

Baxter thought for a moment, then smiled. "I know where you should return them." The wild healer and I looked at our feline companion. "The dark brown side cabinet under the office window," he continued. "There's a space under it. I've seen

dropped papers slide under and disappear before.
You could put them under the cabinet, leaving one
poking out. If he doesn't see them right away, I can
draw his attention to them."

"And he won't find that suspicious?" I asked.

"I doubt it, I mean, I haven't seen him look under
there recently. Then, in the future, I'll keep a nose
and eye out for others."

"That would work well, I think," the opossum
smiled. "Now that I have a place to put them, I can
return them more quickly."

"Perfect." Baxter turned to me, concerned. "I'd
better get you back to you bed, Detective. Like I
said, I don't want to be the one to get you into
trouble."

I nodded, sleepily. "Good idea." I waited while the
opossum and Baxter hefted the furnace panel back
into place. The healer thanked us both, wished us a
good night, and slipped into the darkness. I crawled
onto Baxter's waiting back, and struggled to stay
awake as he glided back to my open recovery cage. I
flopped onto my towel and fell right to sleep.

Dr White checked me out first thing the next
morning. He assured me that nothing was broken,
and that my hoomin would be there soon to pick me
up with an anti inflammatory. I gave my hoomin a
few quick kisses when he reached into my carrier to
pet me. That medicine tastes delicious, and I'm sure

I'll be back to my office in a few days.

The Case of the Compulsive Chewer

My Hoomin took me home from the vet with orders to stay out of my office for a while, and a tasty pain medicine. After two weeks of resting, the boredom got unbearable. My hoomin agreed that I needed a case to work on, but insisted I limit myself to less adventurous problems. The problem was that the pain meds, however yummy they were, fogged my brain too much to work. I started refusing the medicine in the mornings, only taking the evening dose. After a few days, the fog started to lift, and I felt ready to re-hang my shingle and open for business.

I only had to turn away two potential clients. I won't bore you with the details, but I sent one of them off because she made the fur on the back of my neck stand up. There was just something...off...about her. Anyway, I was in my office, trying to avoid either falling asleep or reaching in the drawer for the carrot juice, when I heard a gruff voice from the back door. The pet door only allows certain sizes of critter through, so anything larger than Peanut, the giant bun, has to call from outside. I hopped through the kitchen to the door, and saw a grizzled muzzle poking in under the flap. I told the visitor to make himself comfortable in the shade, and I'd be right out. I hopped up on the table my hoomin left for me so I could look out and assess the safety of the situation. The caller was a very elderly chocolate lab, who shuffled slowly to the far corner of the patio. I watched him carefully lower himself to the cool concrete, and heaved a relieved sigh. He appeared to be the only visitor there, so I climbed off the table and hopped through the door. The Elder dog started to get up as I made my way to him, but I stopped him and assured him that he was more than welcome to relax and rest. He thanked me kindly, and I asked how I could help him.

"Well," he said softly, "my name is Fudge, and I'm the only dog in a house that could almost be called a zoo. There are five rabbits, a hamster, a chameleon, and two parakeets. Our hoomins are kind and loving, and none of us could ask for a better home." I waited patiently while he gathered his thoughts. He shook his head and continued, "A perplexing problem has developed, however, and our people are reaching their wit's end. The mom hoomin has read of your detective skills in Bunnyzine, and suggested that you might be able to help. As the elder, I offered to come see you."

"I'd be happy to help, if I can. Please describe the nature of the problem."

"Hoomins have all these devices that must be tethered to the walls at night."

I smiled and nodded. "My hoomin has a few of those, as well."

"They seem rather common. Anyway, these tethers are constantly being chewed through. Sometimes, as soon as the hoomin connects it to the wall. A few minutes later, pfft, it's been chewed through. I tried to sniff the scenes, but in all honesty, I can't smell so good, anymore. I've asked everyone, individually, if they knew who was doing the chewing, and they all deny any knowledge." He paused, working his memory. "That's all I've got, as far as investigating skills. I hope you can help us."

"I'll be more than happy to help, Fudge. You just rest yourself here, and I'll run in and grab my notebook." I left the elderly canine to relax in the shade, and made my way to my office. I couldn't help flashing back to the Agatha Christie stories that my hoomin read to me when I was little, and I decided that would be the most efficient way to approach this case. I donned my hat and coat, made sure my pencil was sharp, tucked my notebook in my pocket, and rejoined my client on the patio.

I initially declined Fudge's offer of a ride, but he insisted, explaining that the most direct route to his home was across a field of tall grass. He did not need to list the local inhabitants that we might encounter, before I agreed to the ride. I may be a tough guy, but I know my limits against, oh say, a wild fox.

The journey across the field was surprisingly pleasant. Once Fudge got the stiffness out of his joints, he had a smooth, even stride. I even leaned over to snag a particularly juicy stalk of grass. I caught a sniff of fox, about halfway through the field, and pulled off my hat to hear better. Never did see or hear any movement, but I was very glad for the protection my large canine companion afforded.

Fudge and his family lived in a spacious house on the edge of a new development. The large fenced yard had been carefully turned into a bunny-safe haven of green grass and delicious herbs. I slid off his back before he led the way through the biggest pet door I'd ever seen. My initial concern about the possibility of intruders was lessened by a faint beep. The door had a lock on it, and the remote key hung from Fudge's collar. I hopped through the flap, and found myself in a very large kitchen. This place had appliances I'd never seen before. Fudge smiled at my looks of confusion and explained that both of his hoomins were restaurant chefs.

I followed my client through the dining room, and down a set of three stairs into a sunken sitting room lined with floor to ceiling book cases. The bottom two shelves, all the way around, were set up for the enjoyment of small critters. All the way around the room was basically one big bunny playground. The only break in this setup was right by the stairs. A small table was nestled into the corner created by the wall and the stairs. A long bar of power outlets, what my hoomin called a "power strip" was attached to the wall under the table. The strip was full of plastic boxes my hoomin called "power cubes". Only one of the cubes had the remains of a cable sticking out of it. The rest of the cable made its way up to the top of the table, dangling down toward the outlet.

The hoomins had had the sense to cover the power strip's cable with a thick hose. The same kind my hoomin had used for his power cords. I can say from experience that those hoses are thoroughly unpleasant to chew.

With another quick glance around, I put a lid on my inner kit (that looks like a slide, over there...how much fun that would be), and turned back to the crime scene.

I examined the ends of the severed cord. The tooth marks were visible, but indistinct. I'm sure they were bigger than mouse teeth, but that was all the detail I could make out. Whoever had chewed through this had done so in less than three chomps. I put the end of the loose half of the cord right up to my nose. All I could smell was plastic, metal, and hoomin. Why must those hoomins always go out of their way to make my job all that much more difficult? They just have to touch everything!

I sniffed the plugged in end of the cord more carefully. I've been zapped, before, and had no desire to repeat the experience. Again, the smell of plastic and copper, but this time there was an animal scent on the cord. Not enough to tell species, unfortunately, but I was able to rule out Fudge. This cable had definitely been chewed by an herbivore.

Turning my attention to the floor, I scanned around for anything unusual. Finding nothing, I put my nose to the carpet directly under the outlet. I sniffed in ever widening half circles until I reached Fudge's feet. I looked at his languid bronze eyes, and was surprised to see that he was still awake.

"Your hoomins vacuum in here, recently?"

"Yes, first thing this morning."

"Ah, I see. Well, don't feel too bad about not being able to smell anything," I sighed.

His ears lifted in an unvoiced question.

"The hoomins touched the dead end of the cord, and the vacuum got the rest."

"What about the other end?"

"There was just enough there to rule you out," I smiled.

"I'm glad of that," he chuckled.

"So, who are the other suspects, then?"

"Well, there's Charlie, the chameleon. I think we can rule him out, though, since he has never been on the floor, as far as I know."

"Hmm, he's a bug eater, right?"

"Yes, crickets."

"Yup, not him."

"Then there's the birds, Lonny and Lucy. They do come in here, but tend to stay up among the books."

"Might they have seen the perpetrator?"

"Possibly."

"Good. Who else?"

"Next there's Harold, the hamster. He is usually in his ball when he's out, but he knows how to get out of it when the hoomins aren't looking."

I nodded. "And that just leaves the buns, right?"

"Yes. Silky, Snowy, Raven, Arthur, and Pickles."

Pickles? Really? Poor creature. Not that Ears is much better, but at least I HAVE ears. I mentally ran through the list of suspects, considering where to start. The rabbits seemed the most likely, and the parakeets the least. The latter, however, may have had a literal bird's eye view of the crime. One thing I've learned, it's almost always easier to talk to witnesses than suspects.

"Let's start with Lonny and Lucy."

"Okay, their cage is in the Family Room." Fudge stood carefully, and took a moment to stretch. "This way."

Up the three stairs, and across the tiled dining room floor, Fudge lead me into a large living room with plush carpeting. So plush! I could feel my paws sinking into the pile. I looked quickly around to be sure no one was watching, and popped out an experimental binky. The take off was hindered a bit by the deep pile, but it was like landing on a cloud!

Fudge turned to the right and nudged open one side of a pair of glass pane French doors. I followed my client into a large room filled with sturdy, practical furnishings. A children's toy chest occupied one corner, and the melodic chattering of parakeets filled the air. Fudge noticed me looking at the toy chest.

"Our hoomins have nieces and nephews that come to visit. It's easier on their parents to leave a supply of play things here."

"That makes sense. When was the last time they were here?"

"Oh, about three weeks ago, I think."

"Good." I looked up at the very large bird cage, and saw that I was being studied. Fudge introduced us. Lonny, the male, was a brilliant turquoise color with distinct dark markings on his head and back. Lucy, the girl, was covered in vibrant greens and yellows. They were a handsome pair, for sure.

"So this is the famous detective?" Lucy trilled.

"Yes, ma'am, Ears O'Fluffin. Fudge has hired me to determine who keeps chewing the power cords."

"Good luck with that!" Lonny squawked.

"I was hoping you folks may have observed someone under the table. Anyone in the vicinity of the cable?"

"Oh," Lucy whistled, "I know Arthur likes to loaf under that table." She clicked her beak a few times. "But I can't say I've ever seen him bothering the cords."

"Pickles usually goes over, at least once in an evening, to pester old Arthur." Lonny fluffed his feathers as he thought. "But I don't remember him staying under there very long."

"Oooh," Lucy squeaked. "There was a bit of excitement when Harold got out of his ball."

"Really? Was that last night?" I asked.

"Yes," both birds chirped.

I pulled out my notebook and jotted some notes. "What about the other three buns? Silky, Snowy, and Raven?"

"Oh, no. No, no. They all know to stay away from things poking out of walls," Lucy puffed up her feathers with certainty, and Lonny nodded along with her.

"Okay." I put little X's next to those three names in my book. I thought for a moment, then looked back up to the birds. "Can either of you think of anything else that might be of help?"

They both buried their beaks into their feathers, and closed their eyes in thought. After a few moments, they both shook their heads. I thanked them for their help, and followed Fudge out into the living room. I had three names in my notebook. Three strong suspects. And three more witnesses to interview.

Back on the cloud-like carpet, Fudge paused.

"Who would you like to talk to next?"

I considered my three suspects. "How old is Arthur?"

"Oh, well now, I believe he's about eleven years old."

"His teeth still in good order?"

"He eats well enough," Fudge chuckled. "Our hoomins are very attentive of all our teeth. I don't remember ever hearing any concern for Arthur's teeth."

"And how old is Pickles?"

"He's the baby of the family. Barely a year old."

I tapped my pencil eraser on the notebook a few times. "I'd like to talk to Harold, next, if we could?"

"Sure, his habitat is in the Media Room. This way."

At the end of a hallway, an open door led the way down a flight of stairs, and into a spacious basement. At the bottom of the stairs, we turned right and through a short hallway. Another door divided off a large section of the basement for a home theater. On a table behind the reclining chairs, I saw a large hamster habitat. I had to admit that the many twisting tubes looked like a fun place to play, but it seemed odd to have him sequestered down here. I asked Fudge about it, and he explained that Harold liked the cool darkness of this room, and that the hamster was also an avid movie watcher.

Fudge helped me up onto one of the chairs, so I could hop onto Harold's table. No one inside the habitat stirred.

"Hey, Harold," Fudge called. "I brought the detective."

"Go away," a small voice called back. "Sleeping."

"Yeah, well, not anymore, you aren't. Detective O'Fluffin wants to ask you about the cord chewing, last night."

"Hah! I didn't do it. Now go away."

"Harold?" I asked gently. "I was told that you got out of your ball, last night. I was just wondering if you saw anything while you were out that might help."

A reddish tan ball of fur exploded out of the log-shaped hide, scattering paper bedding across the table. Tiny hands gripped the wires, and I was nose to teensy nose with a very disgruntled hamster.

"Did I see anything? Pewps! You wanna know if I did it."

I stood my ground and kept my face straight. "Well, did you?"

His eyes narrowed to the smallest slits, as he glared at me. After a moment, he grunted, "No, I didn't. Not to say I haven't in the past, but I don't fancy the buzz like some critters do."

"I'm not a fan of it, myself. You know anyone who does enjoy it?"

Harold glanced at Fudge, then turned back to me. "I'm not a snitch."

"Of course not, but your hoomins are getting frustrated about all the dead cords. Would you rather they restrict the movements of one, or all of you?"

He twitched his lip about that for a few seconds. "Pickles might, just for the novelty. He's young and kinda silly. But, really, if I had to bet treats on it, I'd say it's Arthur doing it."

"Nonsense!" Fudge interjected. "He's been a house bun long enough to know not to chew the cords."

"You deaf, old mutt!" Harold groused back. "You haven't heard him grumbling about the cords rubbing on his butt. Or the irritating blinking lights. Or the incessant beeping and pinging noises at all hours."

"Humph! I am not deaf!"

"Yer getting' there, ya old coot!" Harold laughed himself into a ball, as Fudge turned away and struck the most dignified pose he could muster.

I watched all this, trying not to laugh along with Harold. It helped to remind myself that I was going to be headed down that road, someday.

It took some effort for Harold to compose himself. I asked my last question quickly, before he could go off again. "Why did you get yourself out of your ball, Harold?"

"Ah, yes, that is the question, isn't it, mister detective bun?"

"Yes, that's the question I asked." I was beginning to enjoy bantering with Harold.

"Alright, I'll tell you the Ham's Honest Truth."

"That would be best."

"I got out to steal Arthur's cookie."

"What?" Fudge whipped his head around, floppy ears swinging.

"Yeah, his cookie. The old fart fell asleep before eating it, and I wanted to get it before Pickles did."

Fudge was incredulous. "Pickles?!"

"Of course, Pickles. You don't honestly think that little pipsqueak hangs out near the old grump because he likes to watch him sleep, do you?"

Fudge considered that for a moment. "Humph! I

suppose that explains why Arthur is always complaining that he never gets a cookie."

"Naturally." Harold narrowed his eyes at Fudge. "And don't you go telling him, either! If he's silly enough to fall asleep before eating it, it's only fair that someone else gets it."

I had to consider that, for a moment. I had to decide if I was going to tell Arthur to guard his cookies better. Being a bachelor (thank Bun! I do not need a dame in my life), it's never been an issue for me, but I can see how it would come up in such a full house. Then another thought came to mind. I didn't want to share it with these two, but decided to ask Arthur about it.

"Well, Harold, thank you. I believe you have been quite helpful." I held out a toe.

"Any time, detective bun. You should come over some time, so we can have a proper chat," Harold stuck a hand out and shook my toe.

"I would like that." I turned to Fudge. "I'd like to talk to Pickles, next, if we could."

I followed Fudge as he made his way slowly up the stairs. I didn't mind the pace, it gave me a chance to review what I had learned, so far. I was pretty sure I knew who the chewer was, and why. After mentally flipping through my pages of notes, I reconsidered my decision to not interview the other three bunnies. I knew I should, just to be thorough, but I

could tell Fudge was running out of energy, and I
didn't want to keep him going longer than really
necessary. I also doubted that they could tell me
anything new. Of course, I might learn something
from Pickles that would change all that.

As we neared the top of the stairs, Fudge paused to
take a few deep breaths. My brain steered itself to
the question of what I would charge for this
investigation. It seemed that everyone was rather
fond of their cookies, so I decided that would be a
good fee. Question then was, how many? That, of
course, would depend on how many more
interviews I had to do.

Heading back down the hallway, Fudge stopped at
the first door on the right. It had been pulled closed,
so Fudge had to reach up to pull the handle down.
The door unlatched with a click, and Fudge used his
nose to nudge it open.

"I'm not allowed in this room, when the hoomins
are away. I'll go in and introduce you, but then I
should wait out here," he whispered.

"I understand." I followed Fudge into the room. It
was a bunny palace. Short pile carpet, perfect for
binkies and sprints, tunnels, digging boxes, climbing
towers, veggie balls, huge piles of hay, and a vast
array of toys filled the large room. "Wow," I
whispered in awe.

"It's pretty nice, huh?" asked a bun so black, she

looked almost irridescent.

Two other buns hopped over to meet us. Up on the tallest climbing tower, I could see a black and white Holland lop, his left ear still not quite fully lopped. In the far right corner, a silvery English Lop loafed on a cushion.

Fudge looked up the tower. "Come on down, Pickles, Detective O'Fluffin would like to talk to you.

Pickles shook himself and started hopping down the platforms of the tower. The three nearest buns introduced themselves. The black bun was Raven. Snowy was a Red-Eye White, whose fur sparkled in the light. Silky was a red and white Rex. All three gorgeous lady buns were giving me their full attention.

"Are you going to interview us, too, Mr O'Fluffin?" Raven asked.

I took a deep breath to steady my nerves (I don't normally get nervous around females, but faced with three at once...I had to force myself not to start fidgeting). "I'm not sure, Miss Raven, that will depend on what Pickles can tell me."

Pickles came bounding over, and stopped next to Silky. I could tell he was getting nervous, so I smiled to let him know I wasn't upset or mad. He smiled back, but edged a little closer to Silky's side.

Fudge pointed his nose toward the back corner. "That's old Arthur. The girls can wake him, when you're ready to talk to him. I'll be just outside the door."

"Of course, thank you, Fudge."

He turned and ambled back out the door. On the far side of the hallway, he gingerly lowered himself to the floor, and appeared to promptly fall asleep. I turned to Pickles and motioned to the other side of the room.

"Will you ladies excuse us?"

"Of course," they all replied.

"Let's talk over here, Pickles." I lead him into the corner. He followed, reluctantly.

"I didn't do anything bad, Mr O'Fluffin, really!"

"We need to know who is chewing on the power cables, Pickles. That chewing needs to stop."

"Yeah, Fudge explained that, but I didn't do it."

"Have you ever chewed a cable, Pickles?" I watched as his mouth screwed around while he thought. "Not just last night, but ever?"

"You won't tell the hoomins?"

"No, I won't tell the hoomins, but if you have been chewing the cords, you can't do it any more."

"I only chewed on one, once. A while ago. I didn't like it, it made me feel funny all night. I swear I haven't chewed any others!"

"Did you go over to Arthur, last night, while he was under the table?"

"Yes," Pickles looked at the floor and started

shuffling his front paw.

"Why?"

"I was looking for his cookie. He doesn't eat them, just carries them over and drops them. Then he falls asleep, and doesn't eat them."

"So you ate his cookie, last night?"

"No," he looked up at me. "Not last night. Harold got to it, first."

I looked at him while I thought about where to go from here. He met my gaze for a few seconds, then returned to studying the floor. I never considered myself as any kind of father figure, but I had a real opportunity to help a young bun, and I couldn't let myself back out.

"Pickles," I waited until he looked up at me. "How often do you and Harold get Arthur's cookies?"

He drew in a deep breath. "Every night." His nose drooped to the floor.

"So Arthur doesn't get his evening cookie, then, does he?"

"No, sir."

"Do you think that's fair for Arthur?" I expected him to make the argument that, if the elder bun wasn't going to eat it right away, then it should be fair game.

Pickles pulled in a breath and opened his mouth. Then closed it. He thought for a few moments, then sighed. "No, sir, I guess it really isn't."

"What does Arthur do when he wakes up and finds that his cookie is gone?"

"He mutters. Looks around the area a bit, then thumps. Then he starts heading back here, still muttering."

I had a pretty good idea, at this point, who was doing the chewing. I also decided that I didn't blame him.

"Pickles," I used the firmest, most fatherly tone I could muster. I waited for him to look at me. "You must stop stealing Arthur's cookies." His ears drooped, but I could tell he was listening, so I continued. "It isn't fair for Arthur to not get his cookie. And if this keeps on, the hoomins might decide to restrict everyone's play time. That's not fair to anyone, is it?"

"No, sir."

"So, can we all count on you to let Arthur have his cookie?"

He sighed again. "Yes, sir. But what about Harold? He takes Arthur's cookies sometimes, too."

"I'll have a chat with Harold before I leave."

"Okay. I'm sorry."

"I'm not the one you need to apologize to, Pickles."

He looked over his shoulder to the back corner. "Yes, sir."

"Good. I'll go have a talk with Arthur, then you can apologize to him."

"Okay."

I made my way through the sea of toys, and approached the aged lop. I grunted softly, and he opened an eye to glare at me. The eye closed, and I thought he'd gone back to sleep. I started a bit when he spoke. "So, this is the famous detective, is it?"

"Yes, sir, Ears O'Fluffin."

"And have you solved our little mystery?"

"I believe I have."

"Well, who was it chewed the cable?"

"You did."

The eye opened again, and I could see just a hint of mirth behind it. "Me?!"

"Yes, sir, you."

"And why would I do such a thing, hmm?"

"In retaliation for the loss of your nightly cookies." He narrowed his eye, so I continued. "The way I figure it, you keep finding your cookie gone, so you try to draw attention to it. They apparently ignore your thump, so you move on to a way to avoid the situation entirely. If no one is allowed to play in the den, you can find a better place to hide your cookie until you're ready to eat it."

The old bun grinned at me. "Very good, young bun, very good. But how do you intend to solve the problem, hmm?"

"I've talked to Pickles, and he has agreed to stop stealing your cookies. I'll talk to Harold before I leave."

"Ahh, so it's those two, huh?"

"Yes."

"Well, then. I doubt you'll convince Harold to stop, he enjoys the challenge of getting out, too much. Don't worry about him, I'll have my own chat with him, this evening."

"Of course. So, you'll stop chewing on the cords?"

"Will I?"

"I think you will, since you know who to confront if your cookie goes missing."

He looked hard at me for a second, then chuckled softly. "Yes, I do. The cords will be safe, from now on. Thank you, Detective."

"Glad I could help, Arthur." I looked back and nodded to Pickles. "Now, Pickles has something he'd like to say...."

"Sure, I'll talk to him."

Pickles hopped over to Arthur, and I made my way back to the door. I was intercepted by the three girls.

"Well, how did it go?" Snowy asked.

"Is the mystery solved, then?" Silky added. Raven just looked at me expectantly.

"Yes, ladies, the mystery is solved. The cords, and you're play time, are safe now."

"Oh, good!"

"So you don't need to interview us?" Raven asked,

her ears drooping slightly.

"Not for this case, Miss Raven, but who knows when another mystery might present itself," I smiled.

A voice behind me almost made me jump. "But we won't be going and creating any mysteries, now will we?" Fudge must not have been asleep, after all.

"Well, no, not intentionally," Raven stammered. The other girl buns giggled.

I bid the ladies goodbye, and followed Fudge out the room and down the hall. On the way to the back door, Fudge opened a kitchen cabinet to pull out my payment. I asked for three bunny cookies, but he insisted I take five. I packed them into my coat pockets, and slipped through the pet door into the back yard.

I couldn't help but pull one cookie out to nibble on during the ride home. Cranberry flavored, one of my favorites. When we got home, I offered to turn on the outside faucet for Fudge to get a drink. He drank his fill and thanked me profusely for all I'd done for his family. I shook his paw, and saw him out the gate.

Back in my office, I pulled the cookies out of my pocket and dropped them in a desk drawer. I hung my hat and coat on the rack, then made my way out to my bed. I decided I'd nap until my hoomin got home for dinner. At least there's no one going to steal my cookies.

The Mystery of the Ghost Ring

The hoomins over at Bunnyzine asked if I've had any spooky cases. I've dealt with my fair share of bizarre mysteries, but only one stands out as truly spooky. More than just a mystery, this is the story of how I found my forever home.

My siblings and I were born in a foster home, shortly after our mum was rescued. I solved my first case fresh off my mum's milk, and was feeling quite proud of myself. Our nest box had a full view of the back yard, but we were safe and snug in the house. One night, my littlest sister had wiggled herself away from the warmth of our pile, so I nudged her back, being careful not to wake her. When I was sure she was a safe, I looked out into the moonlit yard. I froze in place when I saw a tall, lanky man walk through the fence...a solid privacy fence, by the way...and kneel in the middle of the yard. He pulled out a large knife and used it to dig a hole. I watched as he dropped a sparkly object into the hole, push the dirt back in on top of it, stand and walk back through the fence. I stood for a long moment, trying to figure out what I had just seen, when I heard mum's soft voice calling me back to sleep. As I snuggled in with my siblings, I determined to examine the place first thing when the hoomins let us out to play.

After a hearty breakfast, under the watchful eyes of mum and the hoomins, we were all let out into the yard to play. The youngest of my siblings rarely ventured beyond the soft, cozy blanket the hoomins set them on, but mum and a few of us older kits liked to explore. I worked my way through the grass (more like a jungle!) to where I was sure the old man had buried the sparkly thing. There should have been a spot of disturbed grass, but there was nothing to indicate anyone had dug there. I sniffed the ground carefully, and finally caught a whiff of something odd. I started digging. The hoomins made such a cacophony of high pitched squeals (sounds I later learned are called "squee"), that mum came over to see what I was up to. Through the digging, I told her about the old man I'd seen, and that I wanted to know what he had buried. She gave me an encouraging nosebonk, then hopped back to the little ones.

Once I got past the grass roots, I didn't have to dig far before I found the mystery object. It was a ring, like the ones hoomins wear on their fingers, gold with an elaborate insignia and a red gemstone. The

strangest thing about it was how dirty it was. It had
only been there over night, as far as I knew, but it
was caked with dirt. I slipped it onto my right arm
and went looking for mum. She agreed that it had to
have been there longer than one night, and
suggested we wash it off in the big water dish. Once
it was clean, I was certain that it was the object I'd
watched the old man bury. Mum suggested I keep it
on my arm, that it might be important later.

   After a few months, the foster hoomins started
talking about how we babies needed to find our
forever homes. They had decided to adopt my mum,
but couldn't keep all of us. One day, my brothers
and I were picked up by a nice lady hoomin who said
it was time for our big boy operations. We didn't
want to go, but mum assured us it was the best
thing, and would help us find the best forever
homes. The doctor hoomin tried to take off my
sparkly treasure, but I boxed him and thumped as
hard as I could, so he said it could stay. I woke up
feeling quite groggy, wrapped warmly in a towel. I
could hear my brothers nearby, as they started to
wake up. The ring was still on my arm. The next
day, we were taken back to mum to make sure we
healed well. A couple weeks later, we boys were
once again picked up by the nice lady and told we
would be living at the shelter so our forever
hoomins could find us. I didn't like saying goodbye

to mum, but she told me, "Don't worry, sweetheart, you're a strong and brave boy, and I'm certain you will find a wonderful forever hoomin who will love you and take good care of you."

I'm not sure how long I was at the shelter, but no one tried to take my ring again. The first night at the shelter, I couldn't sleep. I felt I needed to look after my brothers, who were able to sleep soundly. Some time shortly after the old clock chimed twice, I heard shuffling footsteps in the hall outside our room. I got up and tiptoed to the front of the hutch, and there was the old man who buried the ring. He smiled and put his finger to the bars. I couldn't smell anything on the offered finger. Somehow he could tell I was surprised because he chuckled softly and whispered, "It's ok, little man. You keep the ring with you, and I promise you'll find the perfect hoomin. Oh, don't worry, he'll know you when he sees you." The old man smiled kindly and disappeared. I snuggled back into my pile of brothers and tried to process what had just happened.

In the next few days, my brothers all found their forever hoomins. The night after the last of them left, I was huddled in a corner feeling lonely. The old man showed up again and talked softly to me. He reached through the bars, his arm passing right through them, and pet me gently on the head until I fell asleep. I leaned over against the back of the hutch, not realizing that the ring on my arm was plainly visible. I woke up to voices in the room. The nice shelter lady was talking to a man with an oddly familiar voice. I didn't bother to move, or even open my eyes, since so many had passed right by me before. Then the voices and movement stopped, and I heard the man right outside my hutch, "How about this little guy?" I opened my eyes and he was standing at my door, looking at me with a concerned expression. The shelter lady answered, "Oh, he's a little sweetie. A bit shy, but calm and friendly. Would you like to meet him in the visiting room?" I sat up and tried to look friendly. "Oh yes, please," the man smiled bigger. I was sure now that his voice was the same as the old man's. Or at least very similar. The shelter lady set the small carrier on the shelf outside my door, and when she opened the door, I hopped straight into the carrier. She squeed and explained that I'd never done that before.

On the way through the halls to the visiting room, the man asked the lady about the ring on my arm. She told him the story of how I'd dug it up from the foster family's yard, and how I refused to let it be taken off. The man spoke quietly to me, pet me gently, and even gave me a piece of pineapple. Yes, this is also the story of how I got hooked on pineapple. The shelter lady handed the man a small

willow ball, and we played a romping game of Toss.
When I was worn out from that, I decided to climb
up in his lap. He scooped me up carefully and
snuggled me close to his chest. He whispered softly
to me, "You know, little man, my grandpa had a ring
just like that." I cocked an ear and looked up at him.
He smiled and continued, "The ring disappeared
after my grandma died, and no one knew what had
happened to it." I wiggled so I could put my right
paw on the man's arm. I let him slide it off my arm.
He examined the scribbles inside the ring and
smiled really big. "Right before grandpa died," the
man was trying to fight tears, "he told me that he'd
buried the ring, but that someday it would help me
find a special someone to share my life with." I
crawled up his chest and gave him a lick on the nose.

   That was almost four years ago. My hoomin still
snuggles me and tells me stories about Grandpa,
who had been a hoomin P.I., and the ring hangs on a
chain on the wall above my bed.